DEDICATION

This book is dedicated to our readers, our family and friends in the present, and those to come in the future. May God always be the Crown Holder in your lives.

TABLE OF CONTENTS

ACKNOWLEDGMENTS

First and foremost, we want to acknowledge Love Himself, who renders all revelation, who inspired us to write this book, and who placed an obedient and outstanding supervisor in our path to encourage us to publish. A sincere, "Thank you!" to Retired Master Sergeant Dawn Ivey-Cochran for giving us the notion to publish.

Secondly, we want to thank our firstborn son, Jaelin Richmond for giving us the time and encouragement that we needed to write, study, and correlate ideas. We love you!

Lastly, we want to thank all of our family and friends who encouraged us to put the pen on the paper, and allow God to speak thru us. May God bless you all!

PREFACE

My husband and I are both from two differing continents where Satan has rampantly attacked the populace monopolizing the most prominent industries, and causing others to follow to their demise. Seeking to follow the direction of God to make disciples, we sought His direction on how to communicate to the world and expose the tactics of Satan.

In excitement, we chose to communicate these subliminal battles by way of an allegory. Throughout the book, we flip thru varying biblical topics to recalibrate minds to the Father's desire for our lives. Our desire was not to create theological rhetoric, but to distribute wise sayings that you should be able to apply to your life.

This allegory was written to expose many messages surfaced within a metaphorical frame, which allows time for laughter, deep thought, and great conversation. It has the potential of being entirely true. However, the characters are animated in a fashion not typical to their norms, neither is it proven that they have or ever will act in the fashion or genders presented in the book; therefore, we have labelled it a fable. Without relying on the scientific and theological specifications, the text can be read times over to discover new truths hidden into its metaphorical skin. I pray that God will richly bless you and spring forth-new revelation to you every time you read this text in Jesus name. Amen.

INTRODUCTION

Have you ever wondered why is it that we struggle in life?

Have you ever interviewed your family and realized that many of you have fallen into the same mistakes? Have you ever wondered, what is God's view on beauty, government, family, our purpose, and many more vast topics? If so, this book desires to help you find answers to your questions.

Daily, we encounter struggles, adversity, trials, sometimes tragedy, but always opposition. In Jeremiah 29:11, God exposes that His plans are always to prosper us, not to harm us, but to give us hope, and a future. How could this be so with so much daily adversity?

Ephesians 6:12 says, "This is not a wrestling match against a human opponent. We are wrestling with rulers, authorities, the powers who govern this world of darkness, and spiritual forces that control evil in the heavenly world."

Those that are warring with us are spiritual beings that sometimes use physical objects or people as instruments to inhibit their plans. In most cases, the spiritual forces that control evil make use of our flesh as their main weapon.

"Someone Covets You?" is an allegory that seeks to expose the tactics that Satan uses to inhibit our flesh to act in opposition of God. The book is narrated by the main character, Sin, but also includes her husband, Death, and her children, Sexual Immorality, Impurity, Debauchery, Idolatry, Witchcraft, Hatred, Discord, Jealousy, Dissensions, Selfish Ambition, Envy, Factions, and Drunkenness. Each character encourages the deed of which they are named. The deeds are defined as follows:

Sexual immorality – Sexual intercourse outside of marriage. Sexual immorality is further expounded upon in Leviticus 15, where God gives the Israelites directions on the proper confines for sex. The scriptures state:

"Never have sexual intercourse with anyone related to you by blood. I am the Lord.

"Never have sexual intercourse with your mother. She is your own mother. Never have sexual intercourse with her. Never have sexual intercourse with your stepmother. She is related to you through your father. Never have sexual intercourse with your stepsister, whether she is your father's daughter or your mother's daughter.

It makes no difference whether or not she was born in your house. Never have sexual intercourse with your granddaughter, whether she is your son's daughter or your daughter's daughter, because she is related to you.

Never have sexual intercourse with a daughter of your father and his wife. She is your own sister.

Never have sexual intercourse with your father's sister. She is your paternal aunt. Never have sexual intercourse with your mother's sister. She is your maternal aunt. Never have sexual intercourse with the wife of your father's brother.

She, too, is your aunt. Never have sexual intercourse with your daughter-in-law. She is your son's wife. Never have sexual intercourse with her. Never have sexual intercourse with your sister-in-law. She is your brother's wife. Never have sexual intercourse with a woman and her daughter or a woman and her granddaughter. They are related. Doing this is perverted. While your wife is living, never marry her sister as a rival wife and have sexual intercourse with her.

"Never have sexual intercourse with a woman while she is unclean during her monthly period. Never have sexual intercourse with your neighbour's wife and become unclean with her. Never give your children as sacrifices to the god Molech by burning them alive. If you do, you are dishonouring the name of your God. I am the Lord. Never have sexual intercourse with a man as with a woman. It is disgusting. Never have sexual intercourse with any animal and become unclean with it. A woman must never offer herself to an animal for sexual intercourse. It is unnatural.

Impurity – A state of being contaminated or polluted. Impurity can be dietary, sexual, mental, emotional, physical, auditory, interrelation, and so on.

Debauchery-Portraying seductive mannerisms. It can be seen in attire, behaviour, interests, forums of expression (such as art or music), etc.

Idolatry- Placing anything superior to God; whether intentional or unintentional. Mankind a

Witchcraft- Merriam Webster defines witchcraft in four ways:

(1) "The use of sorcery or magic"

(2) Communication with the devil or with a familiar

(3) An irresistible influence or fascination

(4) Wicca.

Witchcraft can be performed in many subliminal ways; thru music (in lyrics or encoded speech), artwork, drugs, secret society symbolism, or merely passing off of an object from one person to the next.

Hatred- Extreme hostility or animosity towards a person, place, or thing.

Discord-Disruption of ones state of peace.

Jealousy- The feeling of anger or resentment attached to maintaining what he/she already has.

Fits of rage- Uncontrolled bursts of anger.

Selfish ambition- Focus on things that appear to be to ones' own interest.

Dissensions-Disagreement that leads to discord.

Factions-A segregated group with different ideas and opinions than the larger group from whence they divided themselves.

Envy-Desiring someone or something that belongs to another.

Drunkenness-The state of being inebriated

Orgies-dictionary.reference.com defines orgies as, "any actions or proceedings marked by unbridled indulgence of passions"

The like-Any resemblances to the above fifteen activities.

Throughout this book, we will see Sin from her first approach to coerce Man and Woman onto her pregnancies, her life as a grandparent, business-owner, world power, and ending as a submissive person to the eternal Key-holder.

This book includes many literary forms, but is clearly an analogue of the Bible. There are variations of character uses that differ from the Bible, and the foundational stories have been enacted entwining spiritual and physical characters, which your authors believe to be entirely true in our world, but the majority of people are not aware of these subliminal battles. This book seeks to make the physically unseen presences apparent to our readers.

The following are scripture references used to construct the context of this allegory and should be used alongside to gain greater depth in understanding its biblically constructed foundation:

Genesis 1

Proverbs 16:11

1 Samuel 8

10

Galatians 5

Revelations

CHAPTER ONE:

AN INTRODUCTORY DISCOURSE FROM SIN

"If you do what is right, will you not be accepted? But if you do not do what is right, sin is crouching at your door; it desires to have you, but you must rule over it."

-Genesis 4:7

Dear Reader,

If you are here, it is no accident. Either your curiosity has attracted you to me, or you have heard me screaming for your attention from every high place, and you want a better understanding of why I want the crown in your life. With this book, I will take you on a ride to view my perspective on why I want to be the crown holder in your life.

I have watched in admiration, not just for you, but also for your family; those in the present and those that have preceded you. I sit slavering at the idea of making you feel good. Do you want pleasure? Here I am.

My name is Sin and my husband is Death. Do you think that people get married with aspirations to divorce? Do you think that people try drugs with the motive to be addicted? No. It is not merely the act that you see taking place, but it is I that has taken their minds captive. I have played the lobes of their minds like the strings on a harp; soothing them and making them feel, see, and hear the images that they desire in their innermost being. If you thought that they were captured by the physical illusion, you are lacking intelligence. The true reason for them falling into all-shameful acts are because of me.

It is ashamed that history isolates things that are common to a large populace, but families don't disperse generational history to prevent their descendants from falling in the same traps as they had. For this reason, generational curses are a main tactic that I use once I isolate family vulnerabilities. It's like watching a hamster run in his wheel; I watch your family stumble into the same circumstances as those that preceded them. It does not make sense to me, but I have seen it billions of times.

Do you want to talk about making hell break loose? Don't you love going to the store and spotting a good sale? I feel as if I get an unbelievable sale every time Man or Woman makes a foolish decision (poor choices in relationships, poor music choices, poor movie choices, etc.), and gives me free access to their children. All hell shouts for joy when we find sales like that; buy the adult, get the child for free. I send my daughters; sexual immorality, witchcraft, impurity, and any others that I feel are mature enough to dominate the circumstance. Most of the time, the kids will end up on the same rat wheel as those that preceded them. We have them raped, abused, neglected, introduced to drugs, and the like; resulting in their submission to me forever, and eventually making their permanent residence with Death and I.

Mankind are like sheep; they do nothing that they have not seen done before. If they see women exploiting their nakedness, they will aspire to do the same. If they see others that speak highly of fornication, they will aspire to do that too.

For this reason, I seek those men with power; those that have gained the attention of many. It is these powerful men that I use to manipulate misdeeds.

Every world power has submitted themselves to me, and I have demonstrated my power by controlling them: beginning in Egypt, then Babylon, consecutively moving onto Medo-Persia, Rome, then Europe and America. In the days of old, I enticed men with the same tactics that I use today: cyclic, loveless, substandard sex; a reeking amassing of mental and emotional rubbish; chaotic and cheerless grasps for happiness; knick-knack gods; magic-show religion; distrustful loneliness; cutthroat competition; all-consuming-yet-never-satisfied wants; a pitiless temper; an powerlessness to love or be loved; divided homes and divided lives; narrow-minded and disproportionate pursuits; the venomous habit of depersonalizing everyone into an adversary; frenzied and irrepressible addictions; foul imitations of community, and the like.

After I have made a wrong deed appear to be right by elating a leader, then I pursue his flock, and all of them fall into my uncompromising grip. Man of pure minds, I introduce to ill desires, and sway him to things that infuriate the Father.

Clothes were originally designed to cover the guilt and shame of Man that came during the fall. I have reversed this psychology in the minds of some, telling them, "If you got it, flaunt it! How else are you going to catch eyes?" My ability is beyond that which is apparent to the physical eye, although I use the physical realm to lure man into my spiritual abyss.

For example, in the biblical times I used Egyptian magicians and sorcerers to mock the Father by turning a staff into a snake, water into blood, and performing other comparable magic tricks. When necessary, I can make physical things move to attract men to me.

I tell Woman, "You are ugly! You have to cover your outrageous skin outbreaks!" Instead of running away from me, she runs towards me, and requests my help. Then, I use magic to transform her face. If honesty is what you desire, I will give you a dose.... I HATE YOU AND I HATE MANKIND. I tell my daughter to make man and woman look like I beat them, like they are dying, burning, or simply suffering. She puts black, purple, orange, and all other colours on her face to conceal that she looks like the Father.

Why should they be beautiful? I should be the only beauty. I have recalibrated their minds to desire the things that avail to me. Think about it, why else would Man and Woman like markings of bones, red lipstick, and black eye shadow? I want them to look as if they were beat and lifeless. As with all other tasks, I have directed the sheep into the belief of an ulterior view of physical beauty.

The Father wanted Man to see beauty in virtuous characteristics and to befriend Wisdom beyond all others. He portrayed beauty as love, joy, peace, patience, kindness, gentleness, and self-control. He wanted man to be attuned to the sight of virtuous character thru modesty, humility, diligence, confidence, productivity, dignity, use of discretion in decision-making, generosity, preparation, attentive listening, receptiveness to instruction, and other attributes that the eye can perceive.

Can't you tell a confident person in their stride, or in their tactful dress? Can't you tell a diligent person in the cleanliness of their bodies, and in how well they groom themselves? The Father wanted Man to ally with people of noble character, but on the contrary, he preferred me. Regardless of the plans of the Father, mankind has not preserved their minds, but rather has left the minds as instruments for me to play the melodies that I desire to hear.

You are probably wondering, "Where did I come from?". Good question! I came from Man and Woman's vulnerability. My words are sweet like honey promising pleasure for times beyond what mankind can even imagine.

Since my arrival on the Earth, I have coordinated how to monopolize all earthly industries to include business, science, government, education, healthcare, food, and media; making them submissive entities to my heirs and I.

I have given satisfaction to majority of Earth's inhabitants, so my works are amongst the international norms. Why should my family be in burning sulphur alone? That would not be fair! All men have fallen short. I am simply ensuring that they fall short enough to join my family eternally in the burning, dark Abyss.

In the language, the stature, the lifestyle, the interests, you can tell who is mine. Diseases and sufferings, immoral behaviour, and immodest dress, are signs that I am either working on a sheep, or they are already a part of my flock. These signs are like a bookmark, telling me where I left off, and where to start at my next visitation.

In my wisdom, I show my sheep the water, and put my foot into it, so that they will know to drink. The water may be homosexuality, prostitution, anger, lies, hatred, stealing, masturbation, pornography, or whichever is to my benefit.

I am very professional at identifying when mankind is tempted; it has been my focus for more than six thousand years now. When I examine their area of vulnerability, I direct them to the water that is sweet to their taste. Who wants to be lonely? Who wants to lose things of value? Nobody. My husband and I are like everyone else in that we desire company and we prey after it because it is valuable to us. We are never satisfied with how many we invite into our company, and if we could have them eternally, we would be elated.

Do you have a relationship with God, the gods, or a emulate something in the fashion of a god (nature, science, etc.? I use religion as a pacifier to make people think that they are safe. When the baby cries, I insert it, and distract her.

Want the reality?

There is no safe zone. In the end, you either go to my house or the Father's house. There are no halfway points, gods, or emulations thereof that have keys to my house; they are all in it, so they cannot get you out because they themselves are stuck.

There is only One who has the keys to get you out of my house, and I will speak more on that to follow. If you do not have a relationship with the One who has the keys to my house, then you will be with me eternally.

My plan is the same for you as has been my plan for all of mankind. I plan to be beside you in your most vulnerable and lonely hour. When you have betrayed Wisdom's instruction, I will grab hold of you like the unyielding grasp of lava to those who dare to befriend her, and I will never let you go. You will drown in my multi-faceted cloak, and be adjoined eternally with my husband, Death and I.

Follow me on this continued journey of your life thru my eyes. The remainder of this book will tell you a little bit about my history and how I came to dominate the world. I will introduce you to my empire, and a few stories and tactics that have won us many crowns. With this book, I am hoping to introduce myself in a way that you know how I got here, and if you see me, you will know who I am.

Love, Sin

EXERCISE 1.1

Let's explore the foundations of Sin's role in our lives. We want you to have the ability to identify ways that she may be attempting to steal the crown in your life.

1. Have you experienced opposition that you can attribute to sin attempting to persuade or encroach on your plans?

2. Have you noticed vulnerabilities that are reoccurring in your environment (family, friends, media interests, workplace, etc.)? Example: Mrs. ABC's family and friends all desire companionship, so they listen to music, watch movies, and read books about relationships (usually sexual in nature). As a result, generations of her family and friends' families have fallen into reoccurring sexually immoral acts.

These vulnerabilities (such as a desire for companionship) may not be bad, but when persuaded by sin may be manifested badly. Describe your personal environment vulnerability observations. What could be done to prevent these situations from resulting in sin?

3. Have you seen leaders in government, workplace, churches, etc.? Did you notice the dynamics that this had on their followers? Did this

cause many other people to be confused or to pursue the same immoral acts that they had done? Describe these situations. Pray for your leaders.

4. Do people see your beauty by how you adorn yourself, or do they see your beauty in your virtuous character. It is true that eating practices, hygiene, dress, and other virtual characteristics can be seen with the eye. However, can people see your virtual attributes, or do they see the faddish attire that you maintain?

5. Without words, can people see the God you serve, your values, your morals, and your religious beliefs?

6. Have you seen "religious" people that utilize their religious platform to defend their security in faith or their immoral behaviours?

7. What protective measures are you using to ensure that sin does not receive a buy-one, get-one free sale of you and your child merely for your faults?

8. Have the sins of those that preceded you directly correlated with a behavior that you have or had a hard time to break?

9. Have you noticed an environment that inclines you to fall into sin? List ways in which you can change your environment to ensure that Sin cannot feel comfortable where you are.

10.Think of a person that you consider to have abandoned the sins that you are vulnerable to, and describe the environment that they maintain, the belief system that they hold, and the barriers that they place that cause them not to be susceptible to the same temptation as you are. If possible, spend time gleaning wisdom from this person, so that you can better hedge yourself from environments that cause you to fall.

11. Has your family discussed generational history? How has this knowledge affected your life? Are you more precautious about your behaviour?

CHAPTER ONE PRAYER:

Dear God, I have seen that Satan is constantly seeking for an entrance into my life. I am surrendering my life to you, and I ask that you would help me to change every obstacle that might inhibit sin to grow in my life. Whatever changes need to take place in my life, I am willing because your Word says, "Blessed is the one who does not walk in step with the wicked or stand in the way that sinners take or sit in the company of mockers, but whose delight is in the law of the Lord, and who meditates on his law day and night." I am abandoning the paths that I may take with the wicked, and dedicating my life to meditating on your law day and night. May you bless my life as your Word says in Jesus name. Amen.

CHAPTER TWO

IT ALL STARTED WITH THE POTTER AND THE CLAY

Woe to those who go to great depths to hide their plans from the Lord, who do their work in darkness and think, "Who sees us? Who will know?". You turn things upside down, as if the potter were thought to be like the clay! Shall what is formed say to the one who formed it, "You did not make me"? Can the pot say to the potter, "You know nothing"?

-Isaiah 29:15-16

I guess it would be best to start at the beginning. First, I have to present a disclaimer. My children and I have worked really hard to make some people believe that there can be clay without a potter. Initially, the ideas that matter could evolve from another piece of matter were not sufficient. In times past, individuals would say, "If that were true, where did the original piece of matter come from?"

However, over time, I have been increasingly successful at predominating scientific thought on the topic of creation.

The Big Bang theory, evolution, radiometric dating, carbon 14 dating, and other scientific findings have been a part of my plan. Can science prove anything beyond physical observations?

Have you ever sat a pair of shoes outside, and then watched it disintegrate due to meteorological circumstance?

When determining age, science would be able to use calculations, but no calculation has the ability to determine how many storms occurred during the time the shoes were outside, how direct the sun shown over the life of the shoes, and even worse, science cannot determine what the original state of the pair of shoes were when they were made. The lacking variables make it faulty, however, the idea works for many people today.

Science is entirely dependent on constants. Anything that is not constant (natural disasters, poor construction, or other human factors) is nearly impossible to include in equations such as those used in archaeology and for dating the Earth.

On the up side, I have used the same scientific philosophies (Big Bang and evolution) to diminish the importance of human life. Think about it, if the Earth is millions of years old, you may be one in SEVERAL billion people that walked the Earth. However, if the Earth is thousands of years old, you become a higher percentage of the total Earth's population since creation.

Therefore, the things that you were taught, the things that you teach your children, your reputation, and how you treat other people immediately becomes more important. Just think about it, there are books that date back to shortly after the Earth's creation, which means that some literature has managed to affect a large percentage of the human populace, and it possible for you and I to affect people greatly with our everyday actions.

On the topic of reproduction, I am glad when you are not producing. The first command of the Father was to "be fruitful and multiply". It has always been my task to defy that. I overtly express my sympathy to your economic crises thru my government control tactics (inflation, taxation, etc.)

I deflate godly intentions, and then I shove my pills down your throat. I have used all of my submissive entities to ensure that you stop producing. I tell every nation, "the Earth is over-populated", and "homosexuality is good". Meanwhile, I know that when the Key-holder returns, He will raise all of the dead, and they will inhabit the Earth until His judgment will be complete. How would that be possible if the Earth was not big enough?

Have you seen uninhabited land for sale? I do. Another sign of my success in bribery and smooth talk is that mankind believes that the Earth is over-populated. Eugenics, birth control, and just merely slaying men has been the reaction of men to my words. I do whatever I need to do to please my husband. He is happy to see your babies, even though the Father quickly snatches them from his grasp. Death is happy to meet your loved ones especially the ones that will stay in our house with us forever.

Most people do not think that way, and that crowd is the ones that I try to keep in my company. My son, Dissension does a phenomenal job at heightening the deception on the creation philosophy. Hatred also takes advantage of this topic. Together, they have influenced eugenics, birth control, racism, mass genocide, and many more comparable deeds.

I have to be honest, in the creation account; the original matter had to come from somewhere. Even if masses were to bang together or evolve from one thing to another, it all had to come from an original source. There is the Potter and there is the clay; the Potter is the Father and the clay is everything that you see with your physical eye. If you really want to know how I got here, the true story goes like this:

On the first day of creation, Wisdom was alongside the Father when the first physical object of His affection was bore of His Word, his son Earth.

For three days, the Father nurtured His firstborn son giving him water that would never run dry; so much water that it flowed along his surface, but also streamed from within. The outpour of water that the Father gave His son could never be measured.

He enclosed a hallow of the water to protect and cool his surface (later to be called sky), but also provided an abundance of flowing water along and within his shell to maintain His temperature and irrigate his form. After providing his son with subsistence and ensuring that his thirst would forever be quenched, the Father went onto separate areas that would be dry amongst his exterior from the waters running along his facade (later to be called springs, ponds, oceans, and lakes).

Before long, the Father observed that his son had become somewhat mature and instructed him to bear progenies. As the Father instructed, Earth bore offspring: plants, fruit, and vegetation (later to be named by his brother Man). The Father commended Him, and pronounced His satisfaction with His son and grandchildren saying, "It was good". As the firstborn physical son, he yielded much of the material inheritance and prosperity, but He decided that completion had not yet been reached. The Father continued on to create more offspring that reflected His attributes.

Though the Father was inevitably able to calculate and alter time, on the fourth day he created for Earth a sibling that would help his heirs to mark seasons, days, and would also provide them light. He named His radiant daughter, Sun.

As the Sun was growing in stature and ability, she too gave birth to lesser lights later to be named, the Moon and the Stars.

The Earth was simultaneously bringing forth more offspring: birds, sea animals, and land animals all were born of the Earth. The Universe was growing. The Father was very pleased with

His children and grandchildren, but still had not reached the close of His creation.

On the sixth day, the Father bore a son that possessed His creative, mental, and spiritual attributes and called him, Man. He gave Him a partner, who also bore His likeness, and in astonishment and attraction, man exclaimed, "Woo! Man!"

Due to Man's overt reply, "Woman" became her name, and the two were given the ability to multiply. The Father warned Man and Woman of His desires for them and His plans to always keep them in communion with Him.

He gave them only one requirement. He would say, "Stay away from the prostitute, Sin! Her loneliness is the punishment for her deeds." The Father made Death for me, but did not allow us joy or companionship because of my disobedience, and thus we were to live alone and dissatisfied.

I am perfect in physical beauty. I wear jewellery of every precious stone; carnelian, chrysolite, emerald, topaz, onyx, jasper, lapis lazuli, turquoise, beryl, gold, and others. My voice is a hypnotizing melodic voice that reflects the very essence and majesty of the Father. Prior to my displacement and curse, I would lead the heavenly choir in the melody instructed by the Father; always in perfect harmony. I was the most beautiful of all angels wearing the most picturesque garments; far more elegant than anything known to Man. The Father amassed me with wisdom, and anointed me to entice and coerce all to revere the Father. My perfection made me prideful and I chose to attempt at overthrowing the Father, who is also my Creator, and was therefore overthrown from my prestigious position of great wealth to the Earth.

The Father warned Man and Woman that if they fell slave to my affection, they would lose fellowship with Him, and would experience pain and tyranny as a result. Soon thereafter, Man and Woman intoxicated with my lies and deceit, fell into infidelity; allowing me to distract them from their Father and each other. I lured them into believing that my evil deeds would gain them superior prestige to what their father was offering them.

Up until this point, they were dependent on their Father for food, water, and the provisions for all of their other needs and wants. I introduced the idea that they can become weaned off of the dependency on their father and gain independence by disobeying Him.

I even caused them to believe that they could hold the same authority and power as their Father. Man and Woman invited me into their marriage and into their life. I have lived amongst them as their mistress from there forward.

Soon after my inclusion, I became pregnant immediately; bearing triplets in my first pregnancy. As foretold, conflict began to manifest instantly. As I would caress my stomach, I had already discovered the names of my three babies: Lust, Pride, and Guilt. Competition arose amongst Woman and I to win the affection of Man.

There is no woman comparable to my physical stature. I would visit Woman, and make her aspire to look and act as I do, but to no avail. She would ascertain to my lustrous image, desire for surgical fixes, pray to me even to attain a hint of my scent, but her sights were set on a standard that she would never meet. Meanwhile, I would pursue her man, exposing her flaws to him, and infatuating him with the words, "I can do better than she can. I can make you feel better than any woman has."

Over the thousands of years of my smooth talk, it is still as pleasing to mankind today as it was thousands of years ago. Not only did my physical image make Woman aspire, but Lust kicking in vitro would always remind her that I had more than she did.

Even though she would not always say that she wanted what I had, I know she thought it. However, let me return to my story:

On the darkest night Man had ever seen, I went into labour. Man allowed me to choose the names, and did not revolt. The firstborn son of Man and I, was named, Lust, and then came Pride, and Guilt shortly thereafter.

Promptly when they were born, they had obvious personas. Each of their names came to be defined by their correlating deeds.

Lust was never satisfied. She was the largest of the three, and had the loudest, most unforgiving cry. When I tried to give her breast milk, Lust wanted more food in addition, so I began to supplement my breast milk.

Despite my efforts to appease my new-born baby, Lust always wanted additional, and could never be fulfilled. More than any other diet, she enjoyed candy, sweets, red meats; everything that Man would advise her against, which made her diet a conflict between Man and I. However, Man would always compromise for his families' mutual enjoyment, and to appease his firstborn baby girl.

In addition to her diet being unsatisfied, Lust was a baby that would sleep minimally, and would wail and cry in the presence of Woman. Her sleep behaviours became a huge hindrance of Man and Woman sleeping together. She would sleep for brief periods during the day, but stay awake the entire night.

I also sleep very little and enjoy nights, but Man and Woman were not accustomed to our sleep schedules. They tried to train themselves to different sleep patterns for the sake of their family togetherness.

Notwithstanding Woman's efforts to implore family unity, Lust and I would act very spiteful toward her; Lust would wail and I would
28

attempt to isolate Man from her. Over time, Man and Woman were able to correlate our behaviour with the sight of Man and Woman's affection; we hated it then, and still hate it now.

Lust wanted her parents to show affection, but our affection was in an odd forum; not comparable to Man and Woman. We did not express love toward each other as did Man and Woman. Man and I would only enjoy each other for some ulterior benefit or as bribery of some sort (such as to meet my husband or if Man wanted some material thing). However, Lust was pleased to see her father and mother showing affection, and would make Man and Woman's relationship painful. She became a stumbling block to their mutually beneficial and productive union.

Pride had a very similar character with Lust. He was difficult to satisfy, but rather than desiring tasty foods, Pride desired valuable possessions. Man clung to Pride more than the other two because he was the firstborn son.

Pride had a very sensitive sense of touch and an attention-grabbing voice. Even when Pride was not crying, his babbling was very loud. His volume seemed as if he was attempting to steal prestige from his inception. When I would lay him down to sleep, he would cry if he were laid on cottons or other efficient materials. He demanded velvets, silks, and other materials that were harder to find and produce. However, Man felt that his son was worth the hard work, and would supply Pride with all of his desires.

Guilt was the heaviest of the three although he was not very large. He always wanted to be held by Man and demanded his time. Man and Woman began to have ailments in their bodies because of the heaviness of Guilt. Guilt looked just like me, so every time Man and Woman would look at her face, they would remember me. Woman became disgusted with the three babies, but Man loved them all the more.

With Lust wailing at Man's love for Woman, Pride demanding laborious items, and Guilt requiring non-stop cuddling from Man, he did not have much time to spend with his Father or Woman any longer; their relationships became very strained. I was the only producer of offspring, so Man decided to bear more children of his mistress though his Father had advised him adversely. Man could not keep up with the demands of his growing family, so he was constantly indebted to someone.

His Father told him that He was against the relationship that he had wielded with me, that He would put it to an end, and if He has more children with me, they will cause Him additional agony and malice.

Man disregarded his Father, and bore children with me nevertheless. The children that he and I bore were Sexual Immorality, Impurity, Debauchery, Idolatry, Witchcraft, Hatred, Discord, Jealousy, Rage, Selfishness, Dissension, Faction and Envy. Even though Man was the biological father of my children, they plead their loyalty to their stepfather, Death and I. They had pledged that they would fill our home with Man and Woman's children. My descendants had a shameful appearance, but were very attractive to Man's other offspring, and they interbred into an enormous population.

EXERCISE 1.2

1. What are your beliefs about the creation of the world? Have you founded these beliefs consistently on the Word of God? Is science (global warming, evolution, carbon 14 dating, etc.) fighting the Word of God for the Crown in your life?

2. Do you think that if God desired a child of your womb that you could prohibit it? What is your view on birth control, genocide, homicide, abortion, etc.?

3. Is it difficult to have the faith necessary to believe the words in the Bible?

4. Have you thought about becoming self-reliant instead of praying to God for answers? Have you seen physical evidence of access to something that you desired, and chose to pursue it with your ability instead of waiting on God?

5. Has Sin, Lust, or Pride welcomed themselves into your life? What atmospheres make them feel comfortable? What can you do to permanently alleviate them from your atmosphere?

CHAPTER TWO PRAYER:

Dear God,

I know that You are the creator of the entire universe. I believe that if you could create the entire universe and sustain enough resources for all man, plant life, and animal life that You can definitely provide sustenance to me. I confess that I have fallen slave to sin at points in my life, and I am asking your forgiveness. Your Word says:

"For all have sinned and fall short of the glory of God, and all are justified freely by his grace through the redemption that came by Christ Jesus."

I am requesting the grace of Christ Jesus to redeem me. I am asking that any entrance that sin, lust, pride, or guilt has made into my life be closed, and my communion with you be renewed in Jesus name. Amen.

CHAPTER THREE

SIN USHERS MAN TO DEATH

But now that you have been set free from sin and have become slaves of God, the benefit you reap leads to holiness, and the result is eternal life. For the wages of sin is death, but the gift of God is eternal life in Christ Jesus our Lord.

-Romans 6:22-23

As Lust got older, Grandpa Earth would yield his treasures to her; everything precious that he stored, he would render to his firstborn grandchild. Lust became very wealthy incomparable to every other living being including her dad. She employed many of her siblings, and advised them of how to make great success as her employees.

Despite her favour with her granddad, she did not receive the same preferential treatment from Grandma Sun. Grandma Sun chose things that sparkled when graced by her rays, things that were pleasing to the sight. As did the Father, Grandma Sun preferred to illuminate those things which were truthful, loving, and just, but Lust was only interested in "the things that Man wants". Lust would always flee to the places opposite of where her rays would set.

Her business motto was, "Have what you want, when you want it". Man loved Lust and her intriguing business mission. Her goods were flaunted everywhere in attempts to entice the impulsiveness of Man.

Pride, Guilt, Sexual Immorality, Impurity, Debauchery, Idolatry, Witchcraft, Hatred, Discord, Jealousy, Rage, Selfishness, Dissension, Faction, and Envy were the only individuals hired to hold the corporate responsibilities. Each corporate employee became supervisors of a separate division of Lusts' organization, and their father, Death worked closely with each department.

My family continued to multiply; we hired Mans' descendants, and maintained regular training cycles. Thus, the business became large and full of zeal.

Lust would pair Man with a supervisor dependent on their immoral aspirations. If the employee wanted a love affair, merchandise, property, power, etc., Lust would pair them with the desires of their hearts accordingly.

Each department would entice men to walk in their path. We were most active in our business overnight; lurking, wandering, and looking for Man when he was isolated. If he had company, we would encourage him to isolate himself.

My children have crafty intent, and prostitute themselves to fill my desires. Each supervisor attempts to implement an intimate relationship with Man and Woman to disarm the possibilities for him or her to ever be alone after their first, "Yes".

With persuasive words, we lead mankind astray; seducing them with our smooth talk; until they are completely mesmerized and enchanted by the desires that I had put into their heads.

"I can have what I want now?" Man would say.

"Yes. You can have as much as you want. Just follow me," I'd reply.

In his hypnotic state, I have enticed and deceived him, and as prey to a predator, he is torn away from his Father as meat is torn away from bone.

The Payroll, Marketing, Transportation, and Collection departments are headed by Death, and he ensures retain ability. My husband is strong, and once Man falls within his hold, he has little chance of being freed of his tight clinch. Each business department forwards their customers and employees' addresses to Death because he is outstanding with ensuring employees and customers return.

He tells them, "You only have one life. Live it to the fullest".

Man typically responds saying, "It's true that I only have one life. I guess I should indulge in every desire of my heart".

Man continues to return to Lust for his vats to overflow with pleasure. If he tries to flee, my husband, Death has guaranteed methods of surveillance and return.

He is very punctual and ensures that employees arrive and depart at an appointed time. If they are not attentive, he takes them off of the clock early. I guess you could call him a crook for clocking them out without their knowledge, right? Well, this is our main philosophy for getting man home, to our house early.

Death ensures that transportation is provided to and from the workplace. Small subdivisions are transported straight to the grave daily.

Sexual Immorality, Witchcraft, Impurity, Hatred, Selfish Ambition, Fits of Rage, Envy, Discord, Drunkenness, Wild Parties, and Idolatry all provide daily tours of our home, which can be entered from the grave.

Unfortunately, there are not enough vehicles to bring everyone back, so many have gotten stuck and must enter the grave daily because of my persuasion.

Let me correct one myth that is common amongst mankind.; I never promise longevity in relationships. The only one that I am eternally committed to is Death. I do not know why man and woman cry over seasonal flings. I allow them pleasure, but it amuses me when I see them crying. Do they really think that longevity and true love are formed thru Lust and Sexual Immorality? No! We can ensure that they have their immediate needs met and have a "feel-good time", but long-term love affairs are not in our plans.

Sexual Immorality provides a very pleasurable ride to the grave. Her vehicles are all luxury, but they cannot seat many passengers. She parks her employees nearly everywhere, and makes you feel incredibly good. The temperatures are elating, and no body part is exempted from her stimulation. If you like to ride along public places, she will drive you, but if you prefer to ride along back streets, she will also take you there. She is very discerning of how to set atmospheres for the married, single, or whatever was your relationship status. I am the songstress so there is always music suitable to her deeds. Riding in her vehicles distracts most of her passengers from every covenant and promise they ever signed their name to. She is persistent, so if you do not ride with her when she first attempted to get you, she will ensure that you ride with her eventually. She welcomes her passengers to be accompanied by their toys, animals, family members, and whoever else will allow them the best thrill along their ride. However, the more the passengers she transports, the more likely to be left at the grave.

Sexual Immorality and Impurity usually switch back and forth ensuring that their passengers have a ride. However, Impurity's vehicles are conveniently located and easily accessed, but they are not clean.

36

They have what appears to be bodily discharges throughout the vehicles. Other transportation lines would require that passengers cleanse themselves after riding with Sexual Immorality, Orgies, Wild Parties, Witchcraft and the like, but Impurity said, "jump right on in".

He would go slowly to the grave, but leave most of his passengers there. Sickness, Disease, and Infirmity were all subdivisions within his department. The only time that he moves fast is to arrive on the scene of a tragedy or an accident: bringing with him Unclean Thoughts, Sickness and Disease. Most would advertise that Impurity was recruiting for the aged, but he was really no respecter of persons.

Most of the time, I have Impurity, Witchcraft, or Idolatry transport food to Man in addition to transporting employees. We have our girl time as we are pouring in chemicals and "preservatives" into their food. The funny thing is that they never catch onto their disease rates with the epidemiological surveillance because I have slowly been increasing the dosages over the years so that I can avoid spiking their radar. I like what I see.

The majorities are relying on our mixes for their medications and food sources. I am making it so difficult for conservative farmers to keep up with the industries that have submitted to my advice that they are having to hike their prices for their own family survival, most consumers are unknowledgeable about the controversy and unwilling to pay high prices for food that is not mainstream, and natural food sources are dwindling. My strategy for controlling their food is working.

It is so funny to me that mankind is so infatuated with preservation in dietary facets, but when it comes to their minds, they are like prostitutes; open to all. Has Man ever agreed that food should not be covered but rather freely exposed to bacteria for immunities to be acquired?

For example, let's take a can of tuna: would man ever prefer that the top be off rather than to buy it with its hermetic seal? Would Man ever prefer to buy a food package that had been opened and obviously tampered with? I am laughing as I am writing this because it is so funny that this is the case with their minds. I have conned them into believing that by opening the package and allowing all of the bacteria to come in, they will gain immunities. I have enticed women to flaunt their packages for the means of getting a husband, and I have made Man so accustom to seeing the nakedness of Woman that they can never be satisfied in a monogamous marriage.

Pornography, the modelling industry, the media, and industries of this stature are what I use to feed the sheep. The part that is worse about my use of this tactic of deception is that, MANKIND BELIEVES IT! Now that I have broken the mould of preserving the mind, all other strategies and immoral deeds are easily ushered in. Immorality was created for my advantage.

Drunkenness typically is attracted to adult passengers. His vehicles are more appealing than his siblings, and are prevalent in large populations. Long lines are always awaiting Drunkenness' vehicles. His ride is amusing. He drives so fast that the oxygen flow throughout your body is thrown off; giving you a feeling of elation. His cars are so amusing, attractive, and fun to ride that riders become addicted, and step right back in line after they are dropped off.

When he drives to the grave, he has no choice but to leave a lot of people there because so many people were awaiting his thrill. He makes his dad very proud.

Hatred has the most reckless drivers. The vehicles are bruised and battered because they target Dissension, Discord, Fits of Rage, and Envy with full speeds. They have no fear of destruction, but rather direct themselves towards it. Hatred expediently races his employees to the grave, returning only a small amount of them for further employment.

My husband, Death, is a people-person. He introduces himself to everyone; however, he targets my' repeat visitors and hard workers. He pays employees by the currency of carnal pleasure but when they reach the top of our pay chart, he takes them to our mansion; the grave.

Death shows no favour. He is very fair: exacting the same advantages to all. Age, race, gender, or economic status does not cause discrimination within the company of Death. Of all marketing companies on the Earth, Death has surpassed them all: ensuring to meet nearly 100% of its inhabitants. The only one powerful enough to release the clinch that Death holds is the Father who disseminates power to whom He sees fit.

Even people who confess to being loyal to the Father are on our payroll. What they do not know is that though the mansion is large and houses many, there are no amenities. We have no ability to control the temperature, and the inside is filled with burning sulphur. Going inside our mansion is like falling inside a hot lava-filled volcano; devoid of an exit or vindication. No natural resources needed to satisfy Man's needs or wants are present in our mansion, and there is no hope for comfort after you enter.

There is only a small minority of which Death does not have jurisdiction. They are those who have won favour from the Father. He will always render them a route to flee.

Only on rare occasions had Man permanently fled the hold of Death, and this was only so by the rapture of the Father.

No being can measure our square mileage; our home is big enough for majority of Earth's inhabitants, and our goal is to maximize our space occupancy. Many have become our employees, and meet my husband while attempting to please me. However, we are a couple who never can be fully satisfied.

EXERCISE 1.3

1. Have you seen sinful acts that appear positively promoted?

2. Are you tempted because sin appears to be fun and worry-free?

3. How do you avoid the chemical impurities added into our mainstream food?

4. How do you attempt to preserve your mind? Do you avoid certain music, clothing lines, books, etc.?

5. **FOR MARRIED PEOPLE:** How has a lack of preservation affected your marriage? Have you ever found yourself comparing your spouse to an image that you saw broadcasted somewhere? Do you think placing barriers would allow you to sustain greater joy in a monogamous marriage? Do you attempt to pass these barriers onto your children to ensure their satisfaction with their spouses when they reach adulthood?

6. Do you know your sinful desires? Do you have barriers to prevent you from falling into sin? Describe the barriers that you have placed.

7. Have you seen people or personally fallen slave to the acts described within Sin and Death's family business model? Describe the environments that make these acts attainable.

8. Death is no respecter of persons. Have you seen people die as a result of the acts disclosed within Sin's family business? Describe.

9. Will you be clocked out of life inattentively by not knowing or being attentive to the connection between sin and death?

CHAPTER THREE PRAYER:

Dear God,

The Bible says, "Your word is a lamp for my feet,   a light on my path." From this, I know that by abiding in Your Word, I can be free from all of the dark and immoral acts of the world. I do not want to be an inhabitant of hell, and so I ask that your Word be my guide in Jesus name. Amen.

CHAPTER FOUR:

SIN REALIZES THAT HER TIME IS SHORT

"'Therefore this is what the Sovereign Lord says:

"'Because you think you are wise, as wise as a god,

I am going to bring foreigners against you, the most ruthless of nations; they will draw their swords against your beauty and wisdom and pierce your shining splendour.

They will bring you down to the pit, and you will die a violent death in the heart of the seas.

Will you then say, "I am a god," in the presence of those who kill you? You will be but a mortal, not a god, in the hands of those who slay you.

-Ezekiel 28:6-9

Some ask themselves, "why has disaster come to me?". I have been around long enough to tell you that disaster usually means judgment; whether for good or bad. In some instances, disaster can be for blessing preparation, it can be for testing, but it can also be for rebuke. Disaster is never "natural" and it can never be overlooked. Let me give you an example of one disaster that made a HUGE statement to me of how temporal the Earth's inhabitants are:

Approximately 1700 years after the creation, the Father was overwhelmed with pity for the result of His creation had greatly disappointed Him. Disobedience had reached all-time highs, and the Father no longer had compassion on Earth or Man.

As Man, Woman, and I continued to multiply, wickedness grew greater and greater, and no family line was absent from my influence. Thus, the Father continued to grow discontented with Earth and his inhabitants. Every attempt that He made to gain fellowship with them failed.

Despite our offenses, the Father still allowed us the ability to choose. If we submitted to Him, it would be a signage of true love for Him. Without choice, how is true love determined? It cannot be. It is more in the arena of puppetry, so the Father had not made us puppets, and remained true to His creation.

Earth was harbouring and releasing valuables to Man, Woman, and I, so all of our families were included into the Father's plan of punishment. We were so intertwined that no one could be called righteous or clean.

The Father expressed His discontentment to Man saying that His Spirit would no longer dwell among man greater than one hundred-twenty years, but in the interim, He would send an outpour of rain to flood the world. The flood would cleanse the Earth of Man's wickedness.

Man attempted to pass the message on, but I was busy constantly deterring them from the truth. The majority scoffed and made a mockery of Man because his Father's decrees compromised the natural laws. Never before had such a terrifying rain fell onto the face of the Earth, therefore, the idea was easily made humorous to the majority.

At the appointed time, Earth regurgitated water from his core. Outside of the Earth's atmosphere, from an unseen place in the universe (from which the Father sits) poured waters that covered the Earth. So much water had covered the Earth that the mountains were completely covered.

Some say, "what about the birds, they should have been able to live?". While that statement is true, the flood lasted approximately 377 days, and the water had not subsided to allow them to land, so they too perished. The casualties were uncountable, and not enough living beings survived to acknowledge the amount of those dead. Only a remnant of Earth and Man's descendants remained, and it was only so due to their unwavering faith and obedience to the Father's miraculous instructions.

The survivors were directed to build a ship of cypress wood that was to be 450 feet long, 75 feet wide, and 45 feet high. If a person had never seen rain before, how laughable would the idea be that they believe rainfall would occur in such immense measure that the entire Earth would be covered?

Moreover, how laughable would it be to see eight people in your neighbourhood building the largest ship known in history and believing that it was necessary in an area where water had no apparent threat? Do you see how this idea was easily made laughable? Despite it all, there were still a few that persisted. I questioned him saying things like, "Have you ever seen water fall from the sky?", or "God commanded the horizon to separate the waters above from the waters below, why do you think that he would change that?".

Despite my questions and mockery, still eight individuals persisted in faith, and took pairs of animals alongside them. These persistent individuals survived, but everyone else met their demise, and lives with me.

Though I was the proponent of all evil deeds, the Father had not appointed my demise to come so soon. Instead, the flood was His wrath only to be poured out on living creatures, which breathe the breath of life. Therefore, land animals, sea animals, man, and plants were included, but I was not included in this large catastrophic punishment.

When the floodwaters subsided, and Man reunited with his desolate brother, Earth, he brought his children back to him. Animals of every kind were reunited to Earth. Sun showed forth with greater light because of her excitement regarding their reunification and survival thru such a catastrophe. From her rays, came forth a promised child called, "Rainbow". The Father said, "I have placed this rainbow in the sky as proof that never again will I flood the entire Earth.

That catastrophe let me know that I was favoured by the Lord for a time. The Father told me that I would not be free to roam the Earth forever, but that I would one day be restricted to my house. I was not sure how that could ever take place, but His words added further prominence to my pursuit to misdeeds.

EXERCISE 1.4

Satan pursues you viciously because his time is short. Revelations 12:10-17 says:

Then I heard a loud voice in heaven say:

"Now have come the salvation and the power and the kingdom of our God, and the authority of his Messiah. For the accuser of our brothers and sisters, who accuses them before our God day and night, has been hurled down.

They triumphed over him by the blood of the Lamb and by the word of their testimony; they did not love their lives so much as to shrink from death.

Therefore rejoice, you heavens and you who dwell in them! But woe to the earth and the sea,   because the devil has gone down to you! He is filled with fury, because he knows that his time is short."

When the dragon saw that he had been hurled to the earth, he pursued the woman who had given birth to the male child. The woman was given the two wings of a great eagle, so that she might fly to the place prepared for her in the wilderness, where she would be taken care of for a time, times and half a time, out of the serpent's reach.

Then from his mouth the serpent spewed water like a river, to overtake the woman and sweep her away with the torrent. But the earth helped the woman by opening its mouth and swallowing the river that the dragon had spewed out of his mouth. Then the dragon was enraged at the woman and went off to wage war against the rest of her offspring—those who keep God's commands and hold fast their testimony about Jesus.

1. Have you seen Satan savagely attacking you? Describe.

2. Are you prepared for Satan to be restricted to hell, and Christ to return?

3. Read Ephesians 6:10-20. What is your weaponry when you are under spiritual opposition or attack?

CHAPTER FOUR PRAYER:

Dear God,

I thank you for your Son. I thank You for the sacrifice that You gave for me yet I am a sinner. I understand that Satan has been hurled down to earth, and pursues your people viciously. I am standing here praying on my behalf, and interceding for my brothers and sisters in Christ.

Just as the woman in Revelations 12 was given wings to fly to a place for care and protection, I ask that you would be my provider and protector in these times that Satan attacks me in Jesus name. The Bible says, "Truly I tell you, whatever you bind on earth will be bound in heaven, and whatever you loose on earth will be loosed in heaven." I ask that my fleshly desires, Satan, and all the demons that work for him be bound in Earth and in Heaven. I ask that all contracts or access that the Kingdom of

48

Darkness has been granted into my life be cancelled. I decree and declare that You are the Crown Holder in my life in Jesus name. Amen.

CHAPTER FIVE
ALL CREATION FIGHTS FOR
THE CROWN IN YOUR LIFE

"He draws up the drops of water, which distil as rain to the streams;
the clouds pour down their moisture and abundant showers fall on mankind.
Who can understand how he spreads out the clouds, how he thunders from his pavilion?
See how he scatters his lightning about him, bathing the depths of the sea.
This is the way he governs the nations and provides food in abundance.
He fills his hands with lightning and commands it to strike its mark
His thunder announces the coming storm; even the cattle make known its approach."
Job 36:27-33

Now I have introduced you to my inception, I have given you insight on our family business, you understand somewhat why we are so aggressive, I now want to introduce you to what we look like. At this point, we have no physical form. Our communication is strictly spiritual, which can be recognized in the psyche.

Have you ever come up with an idea, and then felt as if you are going back and forth in conversation within yourself? On occasions, this arguing force could be me. I try to make my voice sound like the Father, therefore, many think that they are following the right path because they have listened to me, but in reality, they have not. I can be identified by destruction, downfall, and disaster, which results from any alliance with myself or my children.

My children's names are Sexual Immorality, Impurity, Debauchery, Idolatry, Witchcraft, Hatred, Discord, Jealousy, Fits of Rage, Selfish Ambition, Dissensions, Factions, Envy, Drunkenness, and Orgies. They have each been very productive, and have bore me many grandchildren. Their lineages have now exceeded Man in generations; we bear children younger and are pregnant shorter. We outnumber Man and Woman many times over, and therefore have completely populated the air; over land and water. There is no place on Earth (besides where the Father) is that is absent from my family's company.

Most people expect for me to be apparent in a ghost-like form. However, my typical appearance is completely contrary. The same temporal structure that houses your spirit is the same structure that I use to house mine. You are probably saying, "You cannot live in my skin with me?", but you are absolutely wrong.

My spirit has no physical density and takes up no space. I have the ability to defy all of the natural laws (with the exclusion of those things that the Father has appointed to occur). I can use any creation to house my spirit and so can my children. At times, I use Earth, sometimes Man, Sometimes Woman, and other covers depending on the circumstance.

Sometimes, I free float thru the air to make individuals second-guess the things that the Father has impressed upon them. There is not enough physical covers for all of my family, so sometimes we share, but other times, we just swarm individuals.

Continue to follow me as I disclose to you a recurring dialogue where my family and I have taken control of powerful entities:

During the aphelion, my son Pride was enjoying his grandfather's company. He was speaking with his grandfather who became receptive to his philosophies.

Granddads' intrigue was the open door for me to come in, and thus, I entered His surface, and took control of his mind. As I was fine-tuning, the Earth began to feel as if he was self-sufficient rather than his earlier presupposition that he was co-dependent. His newfound discovery started to expound within his surface so much that he began to rumble and utter his discontentment loud enough that his younger sister, Sun overheard his utterances.

The controversy was far beyond new. In fact, it was one that occurred seasonally; every time the Earth became isolated in his orbit, my family and I would swarm around him, coercing him, and he would utter. For every time one perceives independent accomplishment, my son, Pride is paying them a visit.

"What is it that I have siblings for?" said the Earth.

"My Father has rendered most of His riches to me. My siblings, Heaven, Sun, and Man all see the fruit of their labours thru me."

Though the Sun was quite distant from the Earth, even at 9 million+ miles, she could not help overhearing his grumbling. My son Fits of Rage hurried to Grandma Sun and she became infuriated. Enraged at his complaining she flames with fury and responded, "Every time you get far on your orbit, you start to think that you are self-sufficient. Don't you see that dad has given each of us co-dependent tasks? Without His help, none of us would be able to accomplish anything."

Overhearing the bickering of his grandparents, my grandson, Government decided to slam the anvil and encroach on their

52

conversation. Majority of his nations have advanced in technology, science, judiciary systems, transportation, and other facets that he perceived as giving himself substantial power and ranking. "Neither of you knew what to do with your riches, that is why I am here. I am the child of Idolatry and Man, but despite my youth, I feel the need to chime in on the conversation. You both must admit that I have definitely become the wealthiest amongst us.

Astonished by his remarks, the Earth replied, "This is an adult conversation! The sun and I are thousands of years older and wiser than you. Do you even know what it means to be wealthy?"

"A wealthy person is the owner of lots of property and controller of all of mankind," Government replied.

"Do you know that all of your leaders combined would still be only a speck in my view? All of your high towers, precious metals, and "expensive" things would be as a speck of dust from where I sit," said the Sun.

After a brief pause, Government said, "Like it or not, I am still the wealthiest and the most powerful. I have sent man to other planets successfully, have either of you done that? I have made a way for them to get light regardless of which direction we are tilted or where we are in the orbit. I have formulated a plan to control all things that hold value, receive earnings from them, and become part owner on all of Earth's possessions.

Earth rumbled and groaned in fury. Sun flared with intense heat. The Earth said:

"Since you have become grown in your own eyes, Mr Government, let me tell you something new under the Sun. You think that you are eligible to be calculated against those that my

Father has rendered His choicest possessions? You say that you are rich, but your wealth comes from me.

Diamonds, precious metals, and all the things that you value have come from me. I am the bank of all of your bankers. I hide value as my Father instructs me, and so also do I reveal it to those that He favours as he directs me. You make money from the things that I lend you, but these things are all rendered from my Father."

"Earth you have not even touched on a portion of this little ones' misdeeds. When I let him borrow my light, he tries to charge people for it. Earth, did you know that he uses metals, has people build towers, captures my light, and charges people for it? Where are my royalties?

"Woo! Woo! Woo! Why are you all speaking against me? Man lusted over my mom, Idolatry. Though she is a prostitute, I am still the product of their deeds, and my father loves me. He has asked for me to be in charge, so I regulate all of his inheritance as he instructs me. I have authority because my father has given it to me. Since he is made in the likeness of God, so also am I, therefore, I uphold a law and ensure justice to the inhabitants of the Earth similarly to your Father," said Government.

Disappointed and nodding, the Earth replied, " Everything my Father has given me, I share. He rewards my generosity, and continues to bestow an inheritance on me. I try at all costs to yield to all who invest their time and labour. The thorns and thistles that man must break thru for their yield is entirely their own fault. I am still upset that I have to store them. Why is it that you are so stingy to Man? You know that your Great Granddad loves him, but you are so hard on him without reason. "

"Without reason is definitely the wrong thing to say," said Government.

54

"I don't even make them pay with their labour. Wherever they are, inside or outside, they reap from me. The vitamins that flow from my rays, I give to all of my siblings and their descendants in abundance. Earth, you say that you are generous, but I even yield to you free of charge," said Sun.

"When my dad desired me, Great Granddad told him the consequences.

Around the time that Israel requested their first king, Saul, rather than a theocracy under God, my territory was enlarged. At that point, I was relinquished and permitted to tax Man, charge him for God-given resources, and to impress upon him inferiority because of his submission to his desire to be like everyone else. I have replaced using the scale to measure value, which typically led to gold or precious metal trading because they are the heaviest, and recalibrated Man to trade one of the cheapest and most plentiful resources; paper. Changing the views on value begins with fine-tuning the mind.

"He said that I rule and that he would groan. Just as Granddad said, I have taken my brothers and made them drive my war-wagons, be my horsemen, and run in front of my war-wagons. I have chosen leaders of thousands and of fifties.

I have chosen men to plough my ground, gather my grain, and make objects for war and for my war-wagons. I have taken my sisters to make perfume, work with the food, and make bread. I have taken the best of my dad's fields, vines and olives, and given them to my servants.

I have taken a tenth part of his grain and vines to give to my leaders and my servants. I have taken his men servants and women servants, the best of his cattle donkeys, and use them for my work. I have taken a tenth part of his flocks, and make him work for me. When my dad cries about his bondage to me,

Granddad does not answer because I am the consequence of his evil desires."

"You both are so wrong for the utterances of your mouths! Sun, whether you shine or not, I still have the firstborn inheritance. Dad has given everything precious for me to store," said Earth.

In a sassy tone, the Sun replied, "Without me, what can be accomplished? Value depreciates if you can't see it. "

"I didn't ask for you to shine! There was light before Dad set you in the sky!" said the Earth.

"True enough, but He put me in place with a responsibility. You think that you don't need me, but let me enlighten you on this topic. Without my light, how much fruit can you yield? Without my light, how much gold or silver can be mined? Better yet, your offspring, Fire, cannot even be born without my light! I divide day from night. I tell you the days and years and seasons," said Sun.

Pacing back and forth across Earth's terrains, Government gets even more zealous that he is truly the most powerful of them all. In great confidence, he says:

"You both thought that you were rich, but you are so undecided that all that you store or your net worth loses its value. Your bickering is another reason that I take the reins in this wealth battle. You both are so busy rotating, flaming, and spinning on your own course that your net worth and potential decline because of you are blind and absent-minded."

"You have let little Government come into this adult conversation and disgrace us," said the Sun to her brother. "He feels that we do not know what we are doing because we cannot agree. Why don't you just except that my net worth far exceeds your and Government's combined so that we can advance in pursuing my purpose in life."

56

"Do you really think that I will ever agree to those terms?" the Earth said in great laughter. I employ all of man. I am the business owner of all business owners, the government of all governments, and the bank of all banks," said the Earth.

After a brief pause and some thought, the Sun said, "It is true that Dad has stored a lot of his treasure with you, but he has made your prosperity contingent on me. As husband and wife are contingent on each other for mutual success, so also you need me. Love is the greatest treasure that Dad yields, and He has given it to me.

If it were not for the Love that He poured out on me, I would have burnt out a long time ago. Love is the gift that keeps me giving, and causes me to stay put for your inhabitants to receive my light. My net worth cannot be equated by adding the remainder of the universe together. Neither can your most enduring flames mimic my heat or my light intensity. With all of Government's fortunes, he cannot afford my density; neither can either of you maintain your balance without me."

Jittery and anticipating a pause in his grandmother's speech, Government jolts out, "I am whose employee? Grandma Sun, you have a point, but Grandpa Earth, I am not tracking. All of my men determine value by weight unless I tell them otherwise. For example, I have been spreading the concept of Federal banking for quite some time, and with that concept, I store the gold in my storehouses while I give my Dad and siblings paper in exchange."

"You do what!" Earth exclaimed.

"I give my dad and siblings paper while I find and store all of the other precious metals."

"My Father is not going to be happy about your ideas, young man! That is like robbery! Paper is not nearly as dense, is much more plentiful, more common, and does not equate to the metals that my Father has given us to measure value. He said that honest scales and weights are His, why have you taken His matter into your hands? Who made you authority over value?" said Earth.

Nonchalantly Government listened and replied, "Who will stop me? Dad put the printing press into the minds of my siblings, and we have now used it to make customized papers used to measure value. Besides, you are too stingy with the gold. Thirty-six man-hours is the average that it takes to pry an ounce of gold from your fingers. Man's time on Earth is not long enough to waste so much searching for gold.

Our lifetime is but a vapour, and before we know it, we will be inhabitants of your matter once again. Since we are short on time, I teach my family to climb the corporate ladder that I have built. Stay with the stable things of life. Do not pursue the risky things that my grandparents try to feed you. I am trying to take more of my family's profits to ensure healthcare for all, I want to make life more fair; a place where the rich and the poor are economically equal. You know, I am striving for peace in the world.

I can accomplish this if I continue at the rate that I am going with regulating my family's wealth.

Earth, I wish you were friendlier to me and yielded everything directly to me, so that I could ensure fairness."

"Fairness is an oxymoron! Non-existent. My Father works by way of favour. He knows what you are doing. He tells me to get you in line, so I throw natural disasters all over the worth in attempt to direct you back to Him, but you are so stubborn. Even worse, you have hypnotized the people where they believe that you are sovereign. You encourage them to do wrong.

Haven't you noticed the natural disasters on your right and left? Millions of people are dying because of my grumbling. You're making my surface a place of filth. The concept that man can control their ability to bear offspring; they can marry whomever (regardless of sex) and divorce as they please, even the concept that Dad does not recognize marriage unless you regulate it. Who do you think that you are, young man? Earth spited. "What talent have you put into their hands? What extraordinary abilities can your render Man?

My Father is mindful of Man. All who commune with Him will be able to surpass you in favour. If man diligently obeys Him, my Father will grant him plenty of goods, in the fruit of his body, in the increase of his livestock, and in the produce of his ground. My Father will open His good treasure, the heavens, to give the rain to his land in its season, and to bless all the work of his hand. He will lend to many nations, but borrow from none. And the He will make him the head and not the tail; he shall be above only, and not be beneath," said the Earth.

"Doomsday is coming soon for you, Mr Government," said the Sun. "What happens in the dark will come to light. For now, you walk around with your head held high; sitting amongst prestigious guests at gatherings, but those things are all temporal. The riches that my Father has given are immortal unlike you.

We all have the option to be cleaned up, and re-assigned new tasks, but my Father already has a plan to overthrow you. Until then, man should behold the abundance and generosity that I show them free of charge. Government and Man should be careful to value my brother Earth, and the kindness that he renders them."

"Sis, you are right," said Earth. Man should also be careful not to be caught being defiant of my Father. He is returning soon, and he has warned that it will be unexpected as a thief in the night. All of the talents that they have, they need to invest them, and increase them. If they cook, let me give them food, if they paint, let me yield for them paint, if they build, let them use my trees. My dad will be infuriated if they have not done anything with the innate abilities that they have been given.

"Multiplying their talents doesn't give healthcare benefits," said Government. "It is sometimes absent from the corporate ladder which is fairly risky, and many times does not give the retirement benefits that I promise. Besides, who is better at marketing than me? Who can achieve wealth absent from me?" said Government.

"Wealth is not yours to give, little one. The Universe is my Father's and everything in it. Man can achieve aside from the corporate ladder, absent from healthcare and retirement benefits. My Father has made man work; He has deemed that it will be so for the rest of his life. Therefore, retirement is vanity! It is best for man to entice the favour of my Father, and to pursue His will. It is only by his pursuit of obedience to my Father that man will reap joy from the work of His hands. Utilize his talents, do not get stuck on stability and being complacent, and entice the favour of His Father, then man will reap joy for the remainder of his short days on Earth."

"You better keep your mouth closed about that, old man", said Government.

"You have rotated off your orbit if you think that he is going to keep a secret for your sake!" said Sun.

"What Earth is saying is true. My Father created Man with the strength to overthrow the entire family of Sin. The sickness, disease, infirmity, and temptations that your family has used to ensnare Man are all temporal. The Father will overthrow you all as Earth has said," said Sun.

Upon saying that, roaring could be heard from the heavens. The Father made His presence and power known to Man. The Father whispered things to Man, of which he became paralyzed and awed at the glory of His Father's tone. Man repeated to his brothers that which the Father told him privately saying, "Father is returning to display his fury and wrath. Those that have rejected Him will be destroyed and the land will become desolate.

On that day, Sun and her offspring will not show their light, but will be darkened. Father has said that He will punish us for our evil. He will put an end to the conceit of the haughty, and will humble the pride of the ruthless.

My descendants and I will become scarcer than pure gold; the universe will tremble so much that the Earth will shake from his place because of his burning anger. Our only resolve is to find the Way and restore our favour from Father."

All of creation pleaded with the Father as He rebuked them each for their individual deeds, and the realization became known that temptations, wealth, marketing, strategies, and plans are in abundance, but without the favour of the Father, nothing can be accomplished.

EXERCISE 1.5

1. Did you notice how Pride set in when Grandpa Earth was away and felt self-sufficient? Do you ever fell self-sufficient? Example: "I can do things all by myself; with no one else's help". Explain.

2. Remember the potter and the clay? Read Isaiah 15:16. What can the clay do without a potter?

3. Does the government provide for you in any way? Example: Welfare, student loans, city services, emergency services, wealth regulation, money distribution, etc.). Have you perceived that the government is a sovereign institution because of all of the services that they offer you? Explain.

4. How can you ensure that the views of the government are not your views by default?

5. In what ways can man reap directly from the Earth without relying on the government?

6. God created the value system. In what ways can we sustain the value system in a country that is mainly using paper to represent an object of value?

7. Have you seen people go to extensive heights to ensure fairness? In what ways can God's favour be shown in an atmosphere that manipulates favour to demonstrate fairness? How can you eliminate the "fairness philosophies" from your actions?

8. Factions are also an illusion that Satan may try to present to others if you choose to show favour to someone. How can you show favour without giving the illusion of factions?

9. What are the talents that God put into your hands? Are you using the corporate ladder and avoiding the usage of your God-given talents? How can you ensure that the usage of your talents makes impact in other peoples' lives?

10. Is someone else gleaning from your riches? Your riches may be your property, your skills, your family, etc. How can you ensure that God receives the glory from your riches?

CHAPTER FIVE PRAYER:

Dear God,

I realize that You are the Potter and I am the clay. I desire to dethrone all opponents that fight for the crown in my life. I decree and declare that You are the Crown Holder in my life, and I am calling You "Sovereign". I submit my mind and my heart to You, and I ask that you would clean them both. Make me see and understand things from the perspective of Your will rather than what is commonly broadcasted and perverted publically. Teach me ways that I can reap directly from the Earth and sustain the system of value as you originally created it. Teach me how to give and receive favour as you shown in Your Word. I surrender my talents and riches unto You, and I ask You to teach me ways to use them for Your glory in Jesus name. Amen.

CHAPTER SIX

THOU MUST KNOW THY KEYHOLDER TO BE SAVED

When I saw him, I fell at his feet as though dead. Then he placed his right hand on me and said: "Do not be afraid. I am the first and the last. I am the living one; I was dead, and now look, I am alive for ever and ever! And I hold the keys of death and hades.

-Revelations 1:17-19

I remember the day like it was yesterday; the day when I was at my steepest state of vulnerability. I was violated like I had never demonstrated on anyone before.

It was in the first century A.D., a young man who strongly had a heart for the Father was my utmost target. He was a leader in everything that he did, and in every place that he went.

On many occasions, my family and I had tried to lure this young man into the abyss by tempting His ancestors, then we tempted those that had governmental authority over him, but all these things failed.

At age thirty-three, the young man had become the talk of the land; known for defying space, time, and all other natural laws. I came face to face with him and told him of all of the physical treasures that I would render him if he submitted to my will. At his weakest state after forty days of fasting, I was infesting his mind with ways to misuse his God-given authority, but he prevailed in that test as well.

Every passive effort that I made to add him into the populace of those in my kingdom failed, and therefore, I pursued him with all of my children.

On the night of the Passover feast, I pursued this young man like the fiercest hungry lion stalks his prey; with no mercy. I put Hatred in charge of this mission. I told him that he must submit to me or lose his life. He claimed to be the Son of God, but I knew that if he revoked those words, I had won many lives into my kingdom eternally.

He was the only that had overcome every temptation thrown at him since the fall of man. I had people spit at him, meanwhile; I was telling him the words that I want to hear:

"I was lying. I am not the Son of God. I have fallen into the hands of Sin. What can I do to redeem myself?"

I kept telling the young man, "I told you all that you have to say. It is not hard after you say it. I promise you riches if you just say it."

He would not say what I wanted to hear! Thus, I escalated the hostility and had him beat until every limb of his body had broken flesh. From his figure poured blood; so much that he probably would have died from open sores alone if time had allowed. However, the young man dying with mere scars and the Father appeased was not in my plans. I escalated the hostility towards the young man again.

I had him betrayed by his loved ones to his face. Usually, the flesh by way of a man's feelings can easily prevail over a circumstance. I wanted the young man to see the wickedness of the people (especially those of whom he spent the most time), and defy the Father. I kept asking him, "If your Father made all this evil that you are looking at, are you sure that you want to be loyal to Him?"

The young man still defied me. I had him sentenced to crucifixion by those with his very own blood; the Jews. His own people laughed and made mockery as he stammered, fell, and got back up again time and time again.

He was still pouring blood from every limb, his strength was weaning, and the task appeared too much. However, the young man still succeeded at carrying his cross to the destination for his crucifixion. He hung on the cross for six hours, but even thru the most utmost and severe pain, he still did not denounce his Father or his family who watched him suffer.

Despite all of my efforts to offer the young man pleasure or to temporarily "lighten his load", he refused. His final words on Earth were, "Father into your hands, I commit my spirit", and he left.

My husband was overjoyed to meet him, and shook his hand and welcomed him into our home. It was at this point that things took a complete turn; opposite the direction that we had expected.

The young man was reverenced in our house like we had never seen before. There was no light in our house until he arrived; it was complete darkness. When people saw light, they began shouting and shoving to reach the light. He spoke and his words caused everyone to tremble, their knees became weak, and they bowed (even those whose will was opposed to it).

His words were sharp and painful to my family and I. Though my husband is far stronger than any man on Earth, the young man's words caused him to drop our most valuable possession; our house keys. We all attempted to jump for the keys, but our efforts failed. In our minds, we were jumping for the keys, but our bodies were shackled, and could not actually move to reach for them.

The young man took the keys to our house, opened the door, and took with him all those who believed that he was the Son of God. Many followed him out of my house.

Before he closed the door behind himself, he told us the rules:

"Those that confess with their mouth that Jesus Christ is Lord, and believe it in their heart shall be saved."

No longer could I lure Man to me and know with certainty that my husband could lock him into our house, but now we do not have the keys to lock anyone away. Access to our home is no longer with our permissions.

The young man is now the most talked about, and though I HATE to hear, see, or say his name, He now sits on the right hand of the Father with the keys of Death at his liberty. No one else can release one from Death's grip but Him.

What tops it all off is that He will return to the Earth, and on that day, I will loose my authority over the air, and all creation will bow to Him. As hard as it is for me to shape my mouth to say his name, the name is Jesus Christ of Nazareth. He is the Key-holder. He is the only one that can grant immortality, and He is the only escape from my husband and I. However, if anyone else owns the crown in your life even while you confess that He is the Son of God, you may not be saved, so choose your crown-holder this day. I want the crown in your life, but the truth is that He made it.

EXERCISE 1.6

The most important key to correctly placing the crown in your life is to know Jesus Christ. When he died on the cross, he went and took the keys to death. Eternal life is not controlled other than thru Christ.

CHAPTER SIX PRAYER:

Dear God,

Your word says:

"Those whom I love I rebuke and discipline. So be earnest and repent. Here I am! I stand at the door and knock. If anyone hears my voice and opens the door, I will come in and eat with that person, and they with me. To the one who is victorious, I will give the right to sit with me on my throne, just as I was victorious and sat down with my father on his throne."

I feel as if you have been knocking on the doors of my heart, and I am opening the door, and allowing you to come in. I confess that You are the Son of God, that you raised from the dead, and that You are the blood sacrifice for my sins. I invite You into my life to become the Crown Holder, and to transform me that I might abide in You eternally. Forgive me of my sins and make me clean in You in Jesus name. Amen.

A DISCLOSURE FROM THE AUTHORS

The Bible says in Matthew 18:19,"Again, truly I tell you that if two of you on earth agree about anything they ask for, it will be done for them by my father in heaven.

We have come in agreement with you on all these prayers. We are praying that the will of God be evident in your life, and that He be your sole Crown Holder in Jesus name. Amen.

ABOUT THE AUTHORS

My name is Stephen Domena and my wife is Tiffany Domena. I am twenty-eight years of age, and was born and raised in Ghana, West Africa.

My wife is twenty-six years of age, and was born and raised in Akron, Ohio. Neither of us had ever travelled to the others' country, and I guess you would ask, "How did you meet?" Hold on, our story will follow.

Neither of us was aspiring authors, ministers, wives, husbands, or anything else that we presently walk in as a calling, but God reshaped our views.

It all began in 2003, when God began to show me the woman of whom I would marry. I was nine years old. I said, "God! I am not even thinking about a wife", but His plans were bigger than mine.

Over the course of thirteen years, He continued to show me visions, her ups, her downs, but I still had yet to meet this lady. In 2008, God showed me that I would be in prison. Despite my tears, sorrows, fasting, and prayers, He deemed it that I would be imprisoned for a time.

The imprisonment came to pass when I was directed by God to take a job in Iraq on a U.S. military installation. Let me remind you that I am a Ghanaian citizen, therefore, my time in Iraq with the U.S. military was not a time of liberty to say the least.

I was treated like property at best, and like an animal on occasions. The U.S. Armed Forces is full of varying attitudes, and thus I put up with a lot to maintain my employment.

I cried out to God, "How long! You told me that I am here for my wife, but she is nowhere to be found!"

At times like that, He would show me another vision of her, and my anxiety would again subside.

After three years of having free access to the base, I switched contracts, which no longer allowed me this liberty. On my first day with my new contract, I needed a security officer to escort me around the U.S. Armed Forces high-dollar equipment (airplanes, heavy artillery, and the like). It was August 4, 2010.

The security escorts walked out. It was three of them, but the Air Force lady with a pistol strapped to her thigh had my attention. She stood approximately five and a half foot high with naturally coiled tresses. They all walked up to my forty foot, heavy load truck, and I noticed at once, "It is her!"

She stared intently at my ID card, then walked over to me and asked, "What does GH stand for?"

I could not help, but to laugh profusely. I was overjoyed. The woman that I waited thirteen years for was finally within my physical view. She kept repeating, "Are you laughing at me?"

From August fourth on, we have been best friends, prayer partners, an encouragement to each other, and forever partners.

On August 20, 2011, I married my best friend. Since, we have started a church plant in San Antonio, Texas, a business, pursued school, but most importantly, we continue to pursue God's call for our marriage, our family, and our life.

This pursuit of God's call for our lives has led us to write this book. We have seen and heard many stories of God's chosen people dealing with subliminal battles, but not even knowing where they began. Our pursuit in life is to draw men unto our Lord and Saviour, and we are praying that this book be a foundational part of that journey.

OTHER PRODUCTS BY THE AUTHOR

REACHING OUR HIGHEST POTENTIAL WITH STEPHEN AND TIFFANY DOMENA (ON ITUNES AND STITCHER)

I WANT TO GET MY CHRISTIAN LIFE TOGETHER, BUT WHERE DO I START?

DESCRIPTION: Everyone needs a foundation; without it, one will fall. This book seeks to help you to build your Christian foundation, so that you can be successful in everything that you pursue in life. If your desire is to understand Christ or to be a better follower, check this book out.

DESCRIPTION: Do you want to have impact in your life? A life of stagnancy is not fulfilling, and does not bring joy. Our purpose is to serve others, but who can lead you in that? Who can give you ideas about how to have the greatest impact? This book is about the person that had the most impact in all history. Can you guess who this person is? Check this book out and see.

YOU MAY PERCIEVE THAT I AM SMALL, BUT OBSERVE BEGINNING DISTRIBUTION ON 19 DECEMBER 2014! AVAILABLE FOR PRE-ORDER THRU EBOOK DISTRIBUTORS NOW.

DESCRIPTION: Do you ever look around and feel confused about your purpose in life? Do you ever feel intimidated by those in your industry? Do you understand your individual assignment onthis Earth? All of these questions and more will be answered in *You May Perceive That I Am Small, But Observe*; a book about right perception.

ONE LAST THING...

If you enjoyed this book or found it useful I'd be very grateful if you'd post a short review on Amazon, and visit my website at http://www.mandatorysuccess.com. Your support really does make a difference and I read all the reviews personally so I can get your feedback and make this book even better.

If you'd like to leave a review then all you need to do is click the review link on this book's page on Amazon here:

USA review link: http://amzn.to/1unsUf4

UK review link: http://amzn.to/1qEbGlV

Thanks again for your support!

Stephen and Tiffany

www.ingramcontent.com/pod-product-compliance
Lightning Source LLC
Chambersburg PA
CBHW070351130626
46556CB00007B/3125